ABC
JAMBOREE

This book is dedicated to all the big people
who are helping smaller people learn to read.
The StoryBots love you!

Visit us on the Web!
randomhousekids.com

Educators and librarians, for a variety of teaching tools, visit us at RHTeachersLibrarians.com

Library of Congress Control Number: 2017935854

ISBN 978-1-5247-1869-5 (trade) — ISBN 978-1-5247-1870-1 (lib. bdg.) —
ISBN 978-1-5247-1871-8 (ebook)

MANUFACTURED IN CHINA

10 9 8 7 6 5 4 3 2 1
First Edition

STORYBOTS

ABC
JAMBOREE

Written by Scott Emmons

• Designed by Greg Mako

The StoryBots invite you to enjoy their jamboree
and share in their adventures with the letters A to Z.
Beep is bright and confident. She leads the group with pride.
Boop is always grumpy, though he's gentle deep inside.
There's Bing, who's full of energy. There's joyful, loving Bo.
Bang is just a laid-back dude who's going with the flow.

Bang

Bo

Bing

They're thrilled to have your company. They think there's nothing better.
You'll all be seeing tons of words that start with every letter.
The StoryBots are ready, and they're glad you're joining in.
The alphabet can be a blast, so let the fun begin!

Aa

Avenue A is a street you'll adore.
It's a place to see acrobats, athletes, and more!
You can eat apple pie or an apricot tart.
You can shop for antiques, armadillos, or art.
There's even an animal act on display.
It's all just amazing on Avenue A!

airplane

art

acrobat

accordion

armadillo

BAKERY

apricot tart

alpaca

automobile

apron

athletes

boat

bathing

ball

bucket

book

bun

basket

Bb

birds

blankets

The sun is **b**lazing. **B**reezes **b**low.
The **b**each is where we're **b**ound to go.
The water's **b**eautiful and **b**lue—
just right for **b**athing. **B**oating, too!
We **b**ounce a **b**all that's **b**ig and **b**right.
We **b**rought some **b**uns. We'll have a **b**ite.
We **b**ask on **b**lankets in the sun
and **b**uild with sand. What **b**eachy fun!

Cc

Hooray for the **c**razy and **c**olorful **c**ostumes!
The **c**ritters on **c**ycles, the **c**omical **c**lown!
There are **c**orn dogs and **c**upcakes and sweet **c**otton **c**andy.
It's **c**ool when the **c**ircus has **c**ome into town!

critter

cycle

cupcake

corn dog

crown

cart

camera

clown

costume

cotton candy

door

drinks

display case

desserts

diaper

dumplings

doughnut

dog

dirty
dishes

Dd

We've got a **d**andy **d**iner
with **d**elicious **d**aily **d**ishes.
There are **d**rumsticks, there are **d**umplings,
and a **d**ozen **d**ifferent fishes!
Our **d**esserts are all **d**elightful.
We've got **d**rinks that make you grin.
So **d**on't **d**elay or **d**awdle now.
It's time for **d**igging in!

Ee

We're **ex**ploring the place where the **e**lephants roam.
We're **e**specially **e**ager to see them at home!
Their **e**ars are **e**normous, and so are their trunks.
They **e**njoy **e**ating **e**ggplant in **ex**tra-big chunks.
They're **ex**cellent dancers, we're sure you'll agree.
No wonder they're so **e**ntertaining to see!

eggs

elephants

eggplant

ear

excited

envelopes

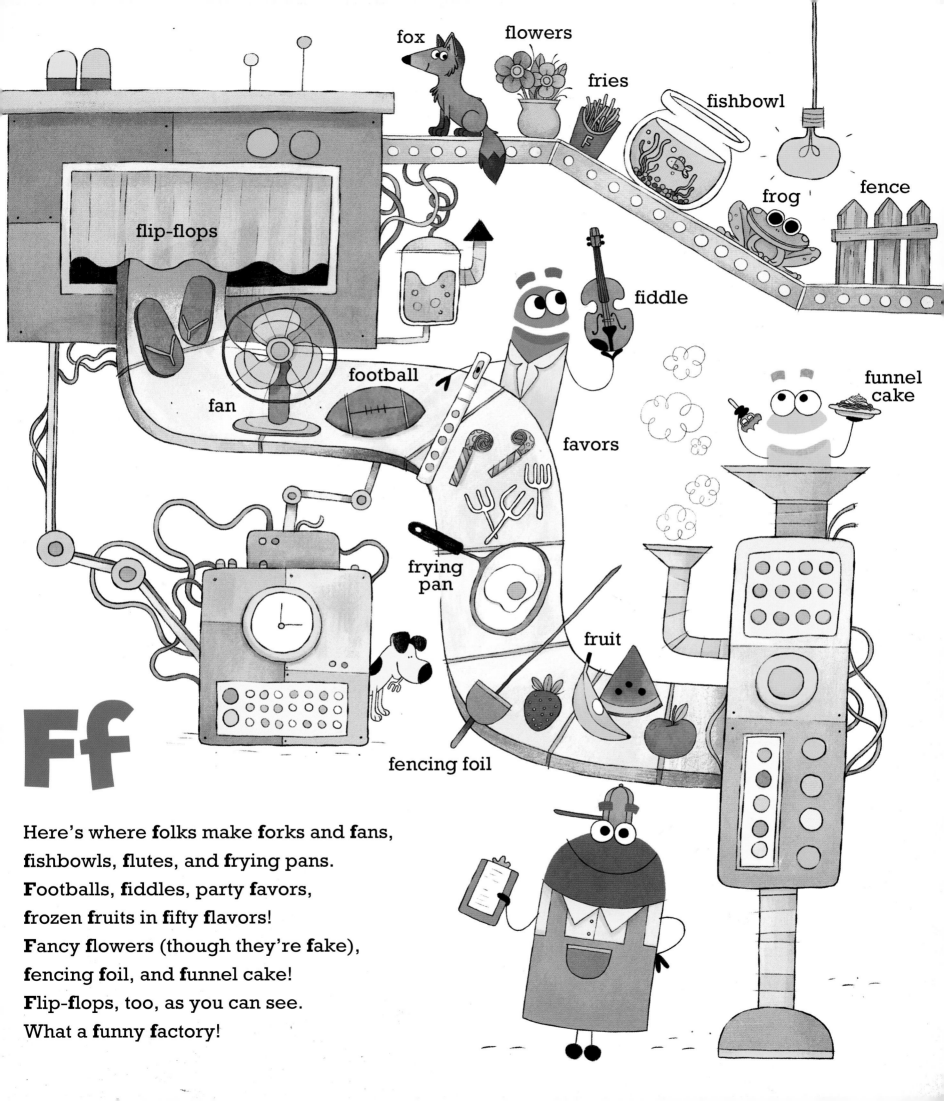

fox

flowers

fries

fishbowl

fence

frog

flip-flops

fiddle

funnel cake

fan

football

favors

frying pan

fruit

Ff

fencing foil

Here's where folks make forks and fans,
fishbowls, flutes, and frying pans.
Footballs, fiddles, party favors,
frozen fruits in fifty flavors!
Fancy flowers (though they're fake),
fencing foil, and funnel cake!
Flip-flops, too, as you can see.
What a funny factory!

Gg

Our **g**arden's as **g**reat as a **g**arden can **g**et.
The **g**randest, most **g**orgeous around!
With **g**allons of water, with **g**loves on our hands,
we **g**et things to **g**row in the **g**round.
Gardenias, **g**eraniums, **g**oldenrod, too.
Our **g**rapes will be ripe in the fall.
The **g**ourds and the **g**reen beans are sure to be **g**ood
if the **g**ophers don't **g**obble them all!

grapevines

gardener

green beans

gate

gourds

gopher

gardenia

goldenrod

geraniums

gallons of water

gloves

glass

hat

hot

hammock

hips

hands

hill

hula

hut

headphones

happy

Hh

It's fun to do the **h**ula
on a **h**ot **H**awaiian isle.
With your **h**ands and **h**ips in motion,
just put on a **h**appy smile.
You can **h**ang out in your **h**ammock
when you want to **h**it the **h**ay,
but for now it's simply **h**eavenly
to **h**ula by the bay.

Ii

I've built a little **ig**loo.
It's ninety **in**ches wide.
Although **it**'s made of solid **ic**e,
it's nice and warm **in**side.
I keep my pet **i**guana here,
my **I**rish setter, too.
But **it** feels a little **in**complete,
so **I**'m **in**viting you.

icicles

iguana

ice cream

igloo

Irish setter

ice

juggling

juice

jam

jeep

jumping
jungle
spider

jaguar

jaws

Jj

Join us on a **j**ungle **j**ourney!
In our **j**eep we often pause
just to see a **j**uggling monkey
or a **j**aguar's mighty **j**aws.
With our snacks of **j**am and **j**uice,
we're **j**ostled when we hit a bump,
and, **j**eepers, what a **j**olt we get
when giant **j**ungle spiders **j**ump!

Kk

In the **k**ingdom of **K**, all the **k**ittens fly **k**ites.
The **k**atydids practice **k**arate in tights.
There are **k**ooky **k**oalas and big **k**angaroos
who race in their **k**ayaks while playing **k**azoos.
The **k**ing beats his **k**ettledrum, shouting, "Hooray!"
It's a **k**ick to be here in the **k**ingdom of **K**!

kites

kittens

knock
knock

katydids

kangaroo

koala

kettledrum

kazoo

kayak

looking

lighthouse

ladder

land

lifeguard

lollipop

lion

loon

lagoon

log

lemonade

LI

We're in a **l**ighthouse, **l**ooking out
and seeing **L** words all about.
Boats that **l**aunch and **l**eave the **l**and.
A **l**azy **l**obster on the sand.
A **l**ifeguard by a small **l**agoon.
Lapping waves. A **l**ittle **l**oon.
A **l**impet **l**ounging on a **l**awn.
And **l**ots, **l**ots more. The **l**ist goes on!

lobster

leaves

lawn

limpet

Mm

We're **m**arching up a **m**ountain
in the **m**erry **m**onth of **M**ay.
We've brought trail **m**ix for **m**unching
and a **m**ap to show the way.
We've **m**et a **m**oose and **m**any **m**ice
and **m**ockingbirds in flight.
Will we **m**eet a **m**ountain lion?
Well, we **m**ust admit we **m**ight!

marmot

mountain

map

trail mix

mountain lion

moose

mice

neck

nest nightingale

noodles

nanny goat

numbers

4121

notebook

newt

narwhal napping

newspapers

Nn

This **n**eighborhood's **n**ot really **n**ormal at all.
It's totally **n**utty and quite off-the-wall!
A **n**ewt with a **n**otebook draws **n**umerous doodles.
A **n**ightingale's building a **n**est out of **n**oodles.
A **n**anny goat's there with her **n**ephew and **n**iece.
Their **n**ewspapers go for a **n**ickel apiece.
A **n**arwhal is **n**apping. **N**ow, that's something **n**ew!
We've **n**ever seen anything like it. Have you?

Oo

ostrich

In the **o**cean there's an **o**rca singing **o**pera for the **o**tters
while an **o**yster grows an **o**rchid in the **o**pen **o**cean waters.
There's an **o**ctopus who's made a little **o**rigami **o**x,
which he'll keep with all the **o**thers in an **o**rnamental box.
The crabs have **o**rdered **o**melets with some **o**lives, black and green,
but an underwater **o**strich is the **o**ddest thing we've seen!

otters

orchid

opera

origami ox

orca

octopus

ornamental box

olive omelets

parachute

pepperoni pizza

picnic tables

pie

pet

Pp

This **p**ark is very **p**opular
for **p**eople and their **p**ets.
With its **p**ines and **p**icnic tables,
it's as **p**eaceful as it gets.
There's a **p**ond where you can **p**addle.
You don't even have to **p**ay.
It's **p**lainly very **p**leasant
and the **p**erfect **p**lace to **p**lay!

paddle

pond

pollywogs

Qq

That big letter **Q** means it's time for a **q**uiz.
Are you sure that you know what a **q**uadruped is?
Just what kind of sport does a **q**uarterback play?
In **Q**ueensland, is **q**uicksand as **q**uick as they say?
And how many ducks make a **q**uacking **q**uartet?
Do you think we should **q**uit with the **q**uestions? You bet!

quadruped

quacking

Queensland

quarterback

quiz

rainbow

redwoods

railroad
tracks

river

rabbits

rubber
raft

ragged
rocks

roses

Rr

Our **r**ubber **r**aft is **r**ound and wide.
The **r**iver's **r**ushing; what a **r**ide!
We **r**ace by **r**edwoods, **r**ailroad tracks,
and **r**abbits eating **r**hubarb snacks.
We pass some **r**oses, nice and **r**ed.
A **r**ainbow arches overhead.
When **r**agged **r**ocks come into view,
we row and **r**ow! Well, wouldn't you?

Ss

The **s**upermarket has the **s**tuff
for **s**alads and for **s**oup.
Spaghetti **s**auces, **s**andwiches,
and **s**oybeans by the **s**coop!
Salsa, **s**pinach, **s**ummer **s**quash.
Salty pretzel **s**ticks.
Uh-oh—**s**omeone had a **s**pill.
Cleanup in ai**s**le **s**ix!

sausages

shrimp

spill

syrup

salsa

spaghetti
sauce

sunflowers

spinach

strawberries

soybeans

squash

tower

top hat

tortoises

teeter-totter

tiger

toys

train

Tt

SCHOOL

TAXI

taxi

Tiny Town has tiny towers,
tiny trucks and taxis, too.
Tiny tortoises and tigers
in a teeny-tiny zoo.
Parks have tiny teeter-totters.
Teachers teach in tiny schools.
When the tiny train has trouble,
workers use their tiny tools.

trees

Uu

UFOs beyond Uranus,
buzzing here and there.
Unicorns on unicycles
in their underwear.
Ugli fruit with ukuleles,
sounding worse and worse . . .
Nothing's unexpected
in this big, wide universe!

Uranus

umbrella

ugli fruit

unhappy

unicorn

UFO

underwear

unicycle

volleyball

van

valley

violets

vulture

vineyard

Vv

It's time for **v**acation! We're off on a trip.
Our **v**oyage begins in our **v**an.
We'll drive through **V**irginia and maybe **V**ermont.
Vancouver as well, if we can!
We'll crank up the stereo's **v**olume and ride.
Through **v**alleys and **v**ineyards we'll roam.
We're taking some **v**ery fun **v**ideos, too,
for lots of great **v**iewing back home.

Ww

When windowpanes grow white with frost,
when winter weather brings a chill—
it's wise to wear your woolly wardrobe.
Winds will make it colder still!

wind

window

wood

wolf

wheels

woodpecker

wool
scarf

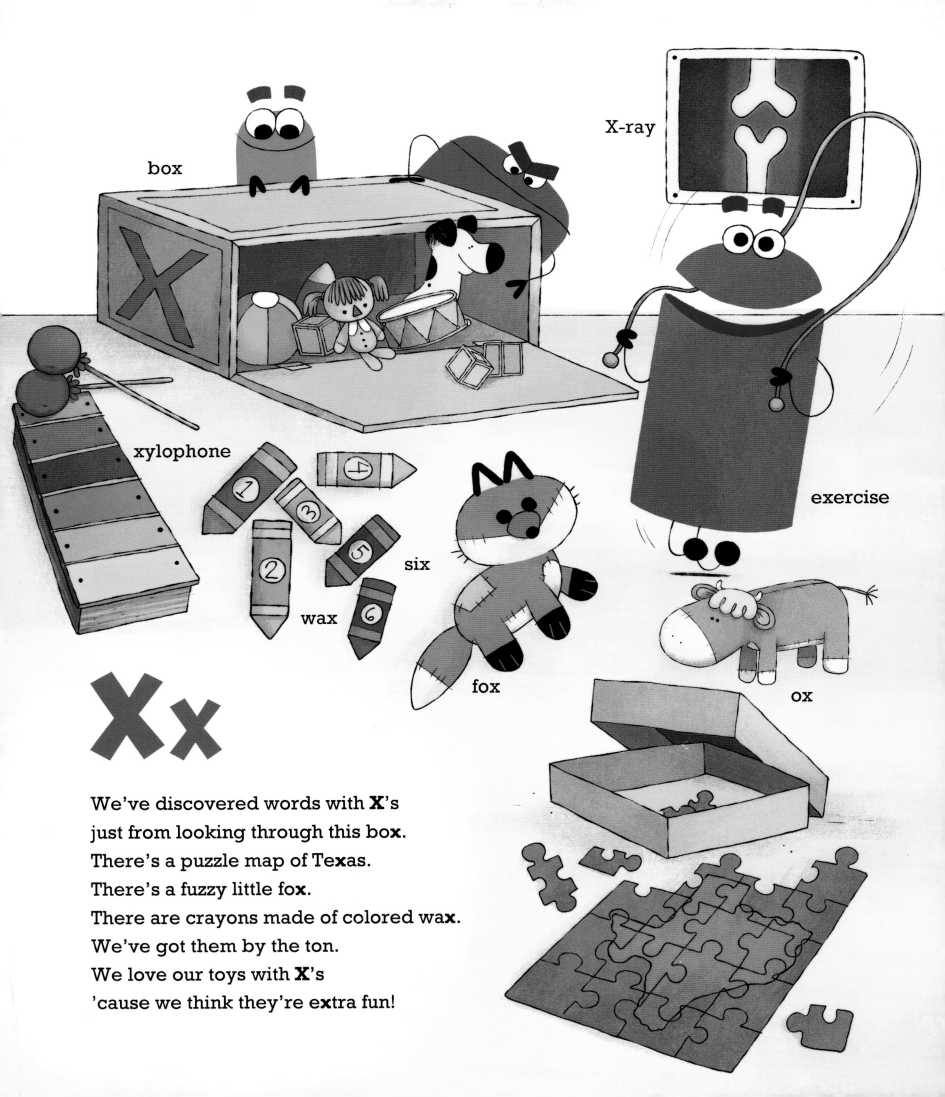

box

X-ray

xylophone

exercise

six

wax

fox

ox

Xx

We've discovered words with **X**'s
just from looking through this bo**x**.
There's a puzzle map of Te**x**as.
There's a fuzzy little fo**x**.
There are crayons made of colored wa**x**.
We've got them by the ton.
We love our toys with **X**'s
'cause we think they're e**x**tra fun!

Yy

The sun is bright **y**ellow. We're **y**elling, "**Y**ippee!
Yo-ho for a **y**acht on the wide-open sea!"
Up **y**onder we'll **y**ield, for a whale's coming near.
We're wishing this **y**acht ride could last a whole **y**ear!

yawn

yo-yo

yak

yellow

yacht

yogurt

zoo

zorros

zorillas

zookeeper

zebra

zebu

Zz

The **z**ebra is an animal
that everybody knows.
Well, what about the **z**ebu?
We can show you one of those.
There's something called a **z**orro
and a striped **z**orilla, too.
If you're fond of **z**any creatures,
come and see them at the **z**oo!

ABC
PICTURE SEARCH

Go back and search for these items,
one for each letter of the alphabet!

Apple pie

Burger

Candy

Drumstick

Eagle

Fork

Grapes

Helicopter

Iceberg

Journal

King

Ladybug

Mockingbird

Net

Oyster

Pine tree

Quail

Rhubarb

Skateboard

Truck

Ukulele

Vase

Wagon

TeXas

Yarn

Zipper